BOTH
PUBLISHING

Published in 2020 by BOTH Publishing.

A CIP catalogue record of this book is available from the British Library.

ISBN - 978-1-913603-08-3
eBook available - ISBN - 978-1-913603-09-0

Printed in the UK by TJ Books Limited. Distributed by BOTH Publishing.

Cover design by Chrissey Harrison and Alistair Sims. Typeset by Chrissey Harrison.

Part of the Dyslexic Friendly Quick Reads Series.

www.booksonthehill.co.uk

AT MIDNIGHT
I WILL
STEAL
YOUR
SOUL

John Llewellyn Probert

**Other dyslexic friendly quick read
titles from BOTH publishing**

The House on the Old Cliffs

Ultrasound Shadow

The Clockwork Eyeball

Anchor Point

The Breath

Sherlock Holmes and the
Four Kings of Sweden

The Man Who Would Be King

At Midnight I Will

Steal Your Soul

The gates were locked.

It was almost all Lynda needed to make her turn round. That and the pouring rain and the darkness and the sheer terror surging through her veins at the prospect of facing a large group of people she had never met before. Her fingers tingled as they gripped the steering wheel of her tiny car.

Her heart, already pounding so hard against her ribcage she was surprised not to be getting any of the chest pains she had been experiencing recently, began to beat even faster as she realised the lane down which she had driven was too narrow for her to turn round. As if that wasn't bad enough, the icy blue display of the car's digital clock reminded her that if she didn't hurry up she would be late.

She hadn't thought it would take so long to find the place. It had been close to dusk when she left the house, the sun gradually being pulled down below the horizon as she drove, streaking the gathering clouds with blood in the futile fight against its decline in the darkening sky. After that it hadn't taken long for the rain to come, the drizzle turning into a downpour just as she left the dual carriageway to join a poorly lit, badly signposted minor road.

Even with the scribbled directions she had been given, sitting on the passenger seat on top of the copy of Bach's St Matthew Passion that she had been told to bring along, and useless now in the darkness, she marvelled that she had been able to find the place.

Not that she was quite so sure now that she really wanted to go there.

She looked out of the rain-smeared driver's window. The cloud cover reflecting the neon from the nearby town meant that she could see, against the fusty orange glow, two high stone walls capped with iron spikes either side of her. There was probably enough room for her to turn round if she was careful, she thought, but if she bumped the car again she'd be furious with herself, and she didn't have the money for any more repairs. Ahead of her, illuminated through a haze of pelting rain, stood two sturdy iron gates.

Two sturdy iron gates with a huge padlock and chain keeping them closed.

She took out her mobile and hesitated for a moment, worried that Dr Sampson might think her stupid for having gone the wrong way, or even to the wrong place altogether, before dialling his number.

It rang twice before he picked up.

"Hi Lynda," said the voice she had come to trust since starting work as his practice receptionist two months ago. "Are you okay?"

She felt herself relax at the sound of his voice.

"Hello Dr Sampson...Richard. I...I seem to have got a bit lost."

"But you're here then?" The voice sounded delighted. "Good girl! That's marvellous. You probably just took a wrong turn somewhere. Do you have any idea where you are?"

Lynda did her best to describe her surroundings.

"Congratulations!" was the reply. "You're very nearly there. You just turned left a little too soon. That entrance isn't used anymore. The best thing to do is reverse until you can turn round, then get back on the road. The main entrance is another couple of hundred yards up on the right. I'll see you in a bit."

Lynda hit the cancel button and looked

behind her. It shouldn't be too difficult to back up and once she was back on the road she could always...

No, she said to herself. You are not going back home. Back to that mother of yours who can't help being old and ill but Oh God her constant complaining is enough to drive you mad sometimes, isn't it? And when she gets really bad, like she was this evening, the one thing you need is an excuse to get out of the house for a few hours. Well this is it, so you're not going back yet.

Besides, Pete might phone and if there is one person in the whole world you want to see less than your mother it's that lying bastard who only sees you when it suits him. Why the hell you even bother with him is anyone's guess. After all, it's not as if he exactly sets you on fire. So you are going to turn up just like you promised, and even if you don't know anyone else Dr Sampson will be pleased to see you. He sounded really happy on the phone that you were coming, didn't he?

He was just being nice, said the other part of her brain. The bad part, the part that tried to stop her doing things. *He would say that even if he didn't really want you there.*

Lynda shut the thoughts out as best she could and threw the gears into reverse. She was going to do this, shit weather, bad directions, and serious state of anxiety or not.

Just as Dr Sampson had said, the main entrance was further down the road. This time the much broader iron gates were wide open and there was a sign that confirmed she was in the right place:

ABERGYFFLAN
PSYCHIATRIC HOSPITAL

She still thought it was a bit of a weird venue to hold a choir rehearsal, but according to Dr Sampson it wasn't easy to find a room big enough for the choral society he had invited her to join to practice in. One of the senior psychiatrists here was a member and he had been able to secure them a slot on Friday nights in the hall that was used the rest of the time as an exercise room for patients who weren't allowed outside.

She drove in and followed the road as it wound down a hill to the car park. Once she had put the handbrake on she took a deep breath. She could still turn back. She didn't have to go in, even though the rain had now stopped.

Perhaps it was a sign, she thought as she forced herself out of the car, slammed the door, and turned to look at her destination.

Quite why the Victorians had built these places to look so bloody scary, she had no idea. Of course that could just be the image they had been given by God knows how many books and films, but it was probably more because she thought that if she was mad and screaming and terrified the building looming ahead of her was the last place she would want to find herself locked up in.

She walked down the hill, pulling her jacket around her and suddenly wishing she'd checked her reflection in the car's rear-view mirror before setting off. Well it was too late now. Besides, her auburn hair, tied back before she'd left the house, still felt tight and neat, and it wasn't as if she'd needed to retouch any makeup.

The security guard at reception told her to follow the signs for Ward 3 until she saw a sign for ECT, at which point she should turn left, then right, then keep going until she came to a fork, where she should take the right-hand corridor and follow the signs for the Rehabilitation Unit until she saw a flight of steps leading down to the left. That was where she would find the rehearsal room.

Lynda thanked him and followed the sign for Ward 3, which was the only part of the directions she could remember. She knew she should have written them down but she had been too embarrassed to ask for pen and paper. With a bit of luck (and when was the last time that had happened, she asked herself) she would meet someone she could ask on the way.

She followed the labyrinthine route through the hospital, trying hard to ignore the crawling sensations in her stomach as she made her way along corridors seemingly lit to maximise the shadowy darkness in their unseen corners. At first it was the emptiness that made her uneasy, but when she realised that if she did meet someone they would most likely be one of the patients she began to pray that she would get there without seeing anyone else at all.

She took two more left turns, a right, passed down a short flight of steps, and found to her delight and infinite relief that she had made it. There was the door on the right-hand side. She grasped the handle, pausing to peer through the frosted glass at the darkened shapes beyond.

Come on, she said to herself. You can do this. Go in.

It took all her strength to push the handle down, and she leaned so hard on it that she all but fell through the doorway.

Hardly anyone noticed.

Lynda looked around the room in which she found herself. To her right were two rows of chairs arranged in a semicircle facing a stage, far away on the left-hand side. Well before that a lectern had been positioned, on which was placed a copy of the work they were to be rehearsing.

Shit! She had forgotten to bring the music! Her legs felt watery as she wondered what excuse to make. She couldn't tell them she had actually remembered it but left it in the car because then they would think she was hopeless. Of course she could always go back but that would mean renegotiating all those awful corridors, and she knew she couldn't face them again alone.

She leaned on the piano that stood near the door, took a deep breath, and tried to ignore the thirty-odd people milling around the room, drinking coffee, chatting, and inspecting their copies of the music she should have brought with her. The fact that she seemed to be the only one without one of the dark green books made her feel even more helpless. She was wondering what to do next when a familiar voice called her name and she looked up to see Richard Sampson walking towards her.

"I'm so glad you decided to come," he said, laying a hand on her shoulder as she gave him a nervous smile.

"Well here I am," she said, biting her lip at how stupid that sounded and wondering if her voice sounded as wobbly

14

as the words felt in her throat.

"Yes, excellent." He handed her one of the green books. "Now you're a soprano, aren't you?" Lynda nodded and took the music. He must have forgotten he'd already given her a copy. She was about to say something but instead she made herself shut up. "In that case you'll be sitting in the front over there. Come on, I'll introduce you to Marjorie. She takes care of your group."

Lynda allowed herself to be led over to a short, jolly-looking woman in her mid-forties who shook Lynda's hand, pointed to one of the chairs and said,

"Why don't you sit there? Things should get going soon. In fact we should have started already but everyone does like to chat! Do you need a coffee?"

Lynda shook her head. The last thing she needed was something that would make her feel even more jittery. She jumped as a tall, bespectacled, academic-looking man clapped his hands and asked if everyone would be kind enough to sit down.

"That's Dr Michael Davies," Sampson explained. "He's the conductor. He's also one of the lead consultants here which is how we get to use this room for free. Anyway, I'd better get to my seat, but I'll see you in the break."

He gave her shoulder another reassuring squeeze and then went to sit down. Everyone else quickly followed suit, Dr Davies taking up his position behind the lectern.

"From the beginning," he said, raising his baton.

The rehearsal began.

Lynda knew the music quite well, which was the only reason she had agreed to Dr Sampson's invitation in the first place. Even so, she found it difficult to concentrate and there were several points over the next half an hour when she let the rest of the choir carry on without her.

Her eyes kept drifting around the others in the room, all holding their copies of Bach's St Matthew Passion aloft. She knew the word had a different meaning in this context, but nevertheless she found herself regretting that so far in her own life she had experienced very little in the way of what could be described as passion, or what she considered passion should feel like. She looked to her right, where there was a broad low window against which the worsening rain had begun to lash. The grounds were lit up and she found herself wondering what the variously sized oblong shadows in the far distance might be, before remembering that she had seen a sign for 'hospital cemetery' on the way in. They were graves.

And there were so many of them.

The music reached a crescendo and she found her eyes welling with tears as she did her best to sing along. Here she was on a Friday night, twenty-five years old and essentially alone in the world, sitting on a crappy plastic chair in a mental hospital, singing a piece of music with the word 'Passion' in the title when she had so far known none, and the only other option she had right at this moment was to look out of a rain streaked window at where people were dead and buried. Sometimes her life felt as if all she was doing was biding her time until she ended up somewhere like that.

Almost as if she was just waiting to die.

For Christ's sake pull yourself together, she told herself as they moved on to the next part. You're no good to anyone when you get like this, least of all yourself. And if you start crying in front of everyone you'll embarrass Dr Sampson, and you don't want that, do you?

Holding her music in one hand she wiped her eyes with the other and then glanced out of the window again.

Where she saw something moving, out amongst the gravestones.

Something that didn't look quite human.

She turned her attention back to the music, only to find her thoughts more distracted than ever. What the hell could it have been? In her mind's eye she saw it again, something that looked a little like a hunchbacked dwarf, limping heavily as it scuttled between the monoliths.

Now you *are* being silly, she thought. If you get any more ideas like that they just might end up keeping you in here. Just take one further look to satisfy yourself there's nothing there. You know you want to and that you won't be happy until you have.

She almost screamed when she saw that the thing was still there.

It had climbed up onto a large upright oblong gravestone and was now hanging onto the top of the marker like a gargoyle. An outsized, even more obscene than usual gargoyle, with a head too big for its body, legs that were nothing more than tiny, atrophied stumps, and arms that were far too long, one of which was wrapped around the wet stone.

It was using the other arm to point at her, the wrist terminating not in a hand but in a kind of crab-like claw that twitched as the thing mouthed something at her through the pouring rain.

She shrieked and dropped her music.

The singing stopped.

Lynda bent down to pick up her score, her cheeks red with shame, having no idea how she was going to apologise for her outburst.

"Morrie? What do you want?"

Lynda looked up. The rehearsal had a visitor. At the same time as she must have seen that…thing (and was it still there? She didn't dare look now) someone had pushed open the door and entered the room. Lynda sat frozen in her chair and regarded the new arrival.

He had to be a patient. Either that or a particularly bohemian gardener, such was his unkempt appearance. Unruly matted hair more suited to a scarecrow than a human being crowned a narrow face whose pitted cheeks had fought a battle with a razor only to lose, leaving a welter of small cuts and tiny missed areas of stubble. When he opened his mouth she was sure the sight would be capable of sending even the most enthusiastic of dentists running in the opposite direction.

"Come to see you, Dr Davies."

His voice made him sound younger than Lynda had originally guessed, the strong Welsh accent giving the words a sing-song rhythm that merely added to his otherworldliness.

"Well we're a bit busy now, Morrie," said the conductor with a weary smile. "If you'd like to come back a bit later we could have a chat then."

The man showed no sign of leaving. He scratched his head and something tiny and black fell from his hair and scuttled across the floor to seek refuge beneath a grey metal cabinet.

"It's just that he's been doing it again, doctor," the man called Morrie said. "Talking to me. He's been talking again and this time I haven't been able to shut him up. I've tried. I really have. But it's the weather, you see? The rain makes him clearer, and with the wind as well it's getting very difficult for me to...stop...him."

Dr Davies reached for the wall phone next to the door, punched three digits and then replaced the receiver. He walked over to the confused young man.

"Look," he said, putting his arm around his patient (much to the consternation of some of the group, Lynda couldn't help noticing), "everything will be all right. Look out of the window."

Everyone followed Morrie's gaze. Everyone except Lynda.

"The storm's nearly over," said Davies. "So that means things should get better, doesn't it?" The man gave a fitful nod that suggested he was not convinced. "Now do you promise me when Dave and Mike come that you'll go with them back to your room?"

Morrie gripped the psychiatrist's arm.

"But Dr Davies, you don't understand! He's been talking to me again! And this time he told me he's going to come back!"

Davies was obviously doing his best to sound reassuring, but if it had worked before it wasn't now. In fact it seemed to be making his patient worse.

"All right, Morrie, all right," he said, trying once more to calm the increasingly agitated young man. "Now look – they're here."

Two burly looking orderlies had arrived. Their faces were kindly enough but they were quite obviously capable of subduing any trouble that might occur. "Now you just go along with Dave and Mike there. They'll stay with you to make sure nothing happens and I'll be along in about an hour or so to check that you're okay."

That seemed to help.

"Do you promise?" said Morrie.

Davies nodded.

"Of course I do," he said. "I just have to spend a little bit more time with all the nice people you can see in this room and then I'll come and make sure you're all right. Are you happy with that?"

Once Morrie had finally acquiesced and allowed himself to be led away, Davies turned to face the choir once more.

"Sorry about that," he said. "It must be the storm. It does upset some of the more delicate patients. We'll just run through the next couple of pages and then I think it's time for a break."

As the singing recommenced Lynda stole another glance out of the window, only to discover that the figure was no longer there. Rather than feel relief, all she could do was wonder what it had been trying to say as it had pointed at her with that horrible claw-like arm.

And where had it gone?

As the break began Lynda had no idea what to do with herself, but she was quickly rescued by Dr Sampson, who introduced her to two friends of his. Dr Fry was a psychologist while Dr McMahon dealt principally with trauma. The two of them smiled politely as Dr Fry said to his colleague,

"Ok – let's see if *she's* heard of it."

"Heard of what?" Lynda said, feeling

her insides cringe at the prospect of some kind of test.

Dr Fry leaned forward, peered at her through rimless spectacles, and in a kindly voice said,

"At midnight I will steal your soul."

Lynda frowned. What the hell was that supposed to mean? Had she heard him correctly?

"I...I'm sorry?"

"Oh don't mind him," said McMahon. "He's just trying to prove that no-one has heard of the film I intend to watch on DVD when I get home tonight."

"No-one's heard of any of the stuff you watch," said Fry. "So I don't see why I should be wasting *my* time with some obscure Mexican film when I could be watching Hitchcock or Bunuel."

"It's *Brazilian* actually," said McMahon as Sampson led Lynda away.

"Sorry about that," he said. "Once they get started talking about that sort of stuff it's difficult to stop them. Come and meet Roger instead."

Roger Wellington was a GP, had more curly black hair on his chin than on his head, and a penchant for biscuits that had presumably contributed to his not inconsiderable girth.

"How are things Roger?" said Sampson once he had introduced her.

"Oh not bad, not bad," said Wellington, trying to conceal the three biscuits he had yet to consume in a chubby fist. "I can't believe we're doing the Passion again. I suggested Faure's Requiem but Michael said it was dreary! Can you believe that? A so-called classical music enthusiast finding Faure dreary! I shall have to direct his attention to the article I wrote in Amateur Choral Monthly. That'll show him."

Sampson gave Lynda a grin.

"Roger's a bit of an academic on the sly. He's written a history of this hospital as well, you know."

"Really?" said Lynda, trying to sound interested.

Dr Wellington nodded.

"I personally prefer the term monograph, although I'm not sure if changing what it was called would have helped sales at all. In fact for a while

I was worried I might have been the reason the local bookshop went out of business. Nonsense of course – it's far more likely it was their refusal to stock all those autobiographies of burnt-out D-list television celebrities." He sighed. "Unhappy endings – that's all people seem to want these days. They love all that 'I shagged around, took drugs, drank myself half to death and now I'm putting on a brave face and pretending to have got through it all but in fact I'm on more antidepressants than all the patients in this place put together'."

"Oh you're just bitter that no-one wanted to buy your little pamphlet," said Sampson with a grin, before whispering to Lynda in a deliberate forced aside, "He's also a big fan of those ghost hunter programmes on the satellite channels, you know."

"Only because they have no idea what they're talking about," said Wellington with a raised eyebrow, aiming his empty coffee cup at the bin. He missed.

"So does this place have an interesting past, then?" Lynda said, to make conversation.

"What mental hospital doesn't?" said Wellington. "But it wasn't always just a psychiatric institution, you know? Years ago all sorts were looked after here, or should I say dumped here when it became clear that little could be done for them. This place became a depository for the deformed, the demented and the destitute. Of course that was years ago, well before you were born. And if you were part of a poor family you might well have ended up here as part of the amusements for the rich and perverted."

"What did he mean by that?" said Lynda as they moved on to meet some of the others.

"Oh just that this place was your typical Victorian Bedlam at one point," said Sampson, clearing his throat and engaging them in conversation with two ladies a little older than Lynda with whom she quickly realised she had absolutely nothing in common. In fact it was a relief when the interval was over and she could get back to the familiarity of her chair.

She picked up her music, sat down, and looked out of the window again. She hadn't had the chance to tell Dr Sampson what she thought she might have seen and now she was quite glad. He would only have thought her weirder than he probably already did, and besides, she wouldn't have wanted any of those other people to hear.

The second half of the rehearsal commenced. Lynda tried to concentrate on the music but her eyes kept being drawn to the window, and to the graveyard beyond. She couldn't get the figure out of her mind. Maybe it had been a child playing out there, in that terrible weather. A child that had now hopefully been rescued from the elements by its parents.

They had only sung a couple of pages when Lynda's attention was distracted by yet more movement, this time from the other side of the door. A familiar wild-haired silhouette raised a hand to the frosted glass to push it open, and as soon as she saw the bitten grime-encrusted fingernails holding onto the handle she knew that Morrie had returned. With an effort he leaned against the door to gain entry and, a little like Lynda had earlier, all but fell into the room.

It was only when one of the other sopranos screamed that Lynda realised she was staring in shock at the bloody smear of a handprint he had left on the glass, and her first impression when she looked at the staggering individual near the door was that he had changed his shirt, replacing the crumpled off-white affair he had been wearing with something dark red.

Except that that the red was dripping.

The blood was coming from a gaping
wound that extended from just below
his right ear, over his neck, and down
across his throat to expose his windpipe.
The tiny, insignificant-looking scalpel
blade that had caused the injury was still
grasped in his left hand while the right
was clasped against the wound. It was
doing little to stem the gushing torrent.

"He told me I had to," he gurgled,
dropping the instrument and leaning
against the piano, tears streaming down
his badly shaven cheeks. "He told me if I
didn't he would steal my soul."

He fell on his face before the choir,
blood spreading across the tiled floor.
Lynda could only watch as people ran

forward to help. One man pulled off his sweater and rolled it up to try and staunch the flow, while the woman behind him slipped in the blood and fell backwards, her skull hitting the floor with a worrying crack.

Dr Davies picked up the phone to call the emergency team, punched at several buttons repeatedly, and then slammed it back down in frustration when the line stayed dead. He grabbed the door handle and pulled.

It refused to open.

"This is ridiculous," he said, tugging harder but getting nowhere.

Two others tried but the door was stuck fast. Davies hammered on the glass but the only noises his efforts made were ineffectual thuds. He took out his mobile phone and cursed. "No signal."

"What are we going to do?" asked Sampson.

"You've got security here, haven't you?" said Marjorie, looking imploringly at Davies. "Someone's bound to come and check on us soon."

"Security doesn't start patrolling for another couple of hours," said Davies. "And Morrie will be dead before then."

"I think it's already a bit late for that," said Wellington, getting up from the lifeless body in front of him. "He must have lost an awful lot of blood before he got here."

Lynda wanted to be sick, but she bit back the nausea. She wasn't going to lose control, because she knew if she did there would be no hope for her.

And no escape from the thing she had seen out there in the graveyard.

She had no idea how or why, but she knew it had to be responsible for what had happened to Morrie, and for locking them in this room, and for making all the phones out of order.

He said he would steal my soul.

She must have misheard him. That was just the title of that stupid film one of those doctors wanted to watch. Maybe Morrie had heard them say it and incorporated it into his delusion.

Or maybe it was because killing himself really had been the only way to save himself from what that thing out there had wanted.

Sampson picked up a chair and threw it at the glass pane of the door. It bounced back and almost hit him. He picked it up again, and Lynda got out of the way as he prepared to throw it against the window behind her.

The result was the same.

"They're all reinforced," said Davies. "This is a long-stay psychiatric hospital, remember? Nothing here is easily breakable."

"What about that?" said Wellington, pointing to an air vent above the door.

"What about it?" said Sampson. "It's much too small for me to fit through, which means you wouldn't have a hope."

"She could, though," said Marjorie. "If

you unscrewed the grating she just might. Then she could go for help."

It took Lynda a moment to realise they were talking about her.

"I really don't know if I could," she said.

"It's only a suggestion," said Sampson. "And only because out of everyone here you're the smallest and slimmest. If anyone can fit through that opening it's you. If Roger and I take it down would you be willing to try?"

Lynda looked at the sea of desperate hopeful faces in front of her, then down at the pool of blackening blood surrounding Morrie's corpse. The corpse that everyone was trying to make a point of ignoring.

"I suppose I could," she replied, having no confidence whatsoever in her ability to do such a thing. But what else could she say? If she refused they would all hate her, for ever and ever. And if they got out of here they would never let her forget it. She couldn't stand that, even if crawling through that air vent meant she might come face to face with—

Don't think about it, she told herself. Just don't think about it.

Besides she might get stuck and—

Just don't think about it.

Roger pushed one of the chairs up against the door and climbed onto it. Unfortunately his bulk proved too much for the flimsy plastic and he only just saved himself from falling as its metal legs buckled inward.

"You'd better let me do that," said Sampson, pulling up a stool and borrowing Wellington's pocketknife. The portly general practitioner steadied him as he opened one of the blades.

He was just starting work on the first of the four screws that held the grating in place when all the lights went out.

The sudden enforced darkness brought screams from the back of the room. Lynda tried hard not to think that it might be because whatever had been waiting outside up until now was getting ready to come in and get them.

"Keep going!" said Wellington when he saw Sampson hesitating.

"That's easy for you to say," said

Sampson. "I can't see a fucking thing."

"Hang on."

As his eyes adjusted to the semi-darkness Wellington got three others to help him move the piano next to Sampson's stool. Then, with the assistance of a leg up he climbed onto the keyboard and then onto the top of the instrument. He fished in his pocket and brought out a pen torch, directing the flickering beam it produced at the panel.

"You're a mine of useful bits and pieces, aren't you?" said Sampson with a grin.

"Comes with the job, dear boy," was the reply. "But I suggest you get a move on as I don't think these batteries are the best."

Sampson was just removing the third screw when the bright yellow glow suddenly became a lot duller.

"Bollocks," said Wellington.

"Don't worry," said his colleague, pulling at the metal. "We should be able to shift it sufficiently to get Lynda through."

Lynda was starting to have second thoughts, not least because during their efforts she had ended up sitting next to Dr Davies.

"I should have listened, I suppose," he said, to no-one in particular. "Paid more attention."

"I'm sure you listened to Morrie more than anyone," she said.

"Not Morrie," he replied, turning to her.

"The others."

Lynda didn't really want to know but before she could stop herself she had already asked what he meant.

"You mean you haven't heard?" he said. "Perhaps you don't read the local press. Over the last month patients here have been behaving out of character, aside from their diagnosed conditions. Some have even been mutilating themselves, and not just the ones who are in here for deliberate self-harm. We've had to deep clean seven of the rooms in the last fortnight because of what's ended up on the walls. The carpets have all had to be ripped out as well."

"You've had seven patients injure themselves so badly they've bled all over the walls and floors of their rooms?" said Lynda, her face aghast in the gloom.

Davies gave her a furtive glance.

"Only a couple of them," he said. "The rest, well, let's just say it's possible to make an awful mess of a room with just about any kind of bodily fluid. I'm sure you understand."

Lynda didn't, not really, and she didn't even want to try. In fact she was glad when she heard Sampson call her name.

"I think we're ready to try now," he said.

She got to her feet and tried to put on a brave face. No-one would be able to see it in the dark but it made her feel better and at the moment that was what was important.

"Have a look and see if you can get through," said Sampson, jumping down.

Lynda climbed onto the stool and peered into the narrow space. She could just see the corridor on the other side of the door.

"Do you think you can make it?" Wellington called up.

"I think so," she said. "But I'm not sure if I can remember the way back to the main entrance."

"You shouldn't need to," said Sampson. "Just keep going until you find someone who can let us out."

"Okay," she said, placing her hands on the vent and bracing herself for them to lift her up. Suddenly a thought struck her, something that she realised she had to ask before it was too late. She looked down at Wellington.

"You said you wrote a book on the history of this place," she said.

"Monograph," he said with a grin. "Yes, why?"

"I just wanted to check I'm not going to bump into any ghosts out there."

Wellington said nothing.

Sampson prodded him.

"She said she hoped that—"

"I know what she said!" The confidence had gone from Wellington's voice and he suddenly sounded even more frightened than she was. She wished she hadn't asked him as Wellington handed her the pen torch and then the two men grabbed her legs and lifted her up.

"Just as long as it's nothing to do with a hideous dwarf or anything like that," she said as she squeezed through.

"Well it's odd you should mention that," said Wellington.

"Shut up, Roger," Lynda heard Sampson say from behind her. "The last thing she needs is to hear you waffling on about that sort of rubbish."

"I merely wanted to point out that no-one *has* ever seen a dwarf," Wellington continued, "but that just makes it all the more interesting because with every reported ghost sighting each individual has claimed to see something completely different from everyone else. Lynda? Have *you* seen something?"

But the voices behind her were already fading as she pulled herself through the vent, the narrow passage constricting her too severely for her to be able to shout a reply as her head emerged from the other side. Her body was about halfway out when gravity took over and she fell to the ground, her outstretched arms saving her head from a nasty smack against the cold floor.

She got to her feet, and for a moment all she could feel was the triumph of success.

"I'm through!" she said.

There was no sound from the other side.

Lynda put her face close to the door and shouted.

"Can you hear me? I'm through!"

Nothing.

She frowned. Surely the door couldn't be so thick as to prevent the passage of any sound at all? She rapped on the glass, to be rewarded with the same dull thud that had greeted Dr Davies' attempts.

That had to be the answer, she thought. They couldn't have all just disappeared, although that still didn't explain why sound of their voices couldn't have been carried through the air vent.

She looked up. In the gloom it looked as if the hole through which she had just emerged had vanished. Which was nonsense, of course.

She wished she had been able to

hear more of what Dr Wellington had been going to say, but perhaps she was better off hearing it when they were all safely out of there. Besides, now she knew there were stories about this place she felt a little better in a strange way – she must have either read about them somewhere, or overheard someone talking about them, and that, combined with her overactive imagination, must have led to her seeing the thing in the graveyard.

In fact the more she thought about it the more she remembered the time she had seen something similar, at a fairground ride she had been taken on as a little girl. She hadn't wanted to go but her father, who had quite obviously wanted a boy from the way he had insisted she accompany him to football games and on his fishing trips despite her reticence, had said no daughter of his was going to grow up scared of smoke and mirrors.

She had been terrified.

And the worst had been reserved for the very end, when the ride was meant to be over and she had thought she could relax. Then she had seen it.

Of course it hadn't turned out to be a twisted, hunchbacked dwarf with a claw for a hand at all, but one of the maintenance men bent over adjusting the bearings on the side of the track on the way out. But as he had turned to face the carriage in which she and her father had been riding, his bent over form in silhouette, the wrench he had been holding in his right hand resembling a ghastly pincer-like appendage, it had been enough to cause her to have hysterics, much to the embarrassment and anger of the man she looked up to. She had been dragged screaming away from the ride, taken home, and punished. It had been one of the worst days of her life.

She shook her head. Now wasn't the time to begin dredging up old terrors. She had to help all those people who were still trapped.

Even though there were still no sounds from the room behind her.

And no movement, either.

She took the pen torch Dr Wellington had thrust into her hand and shone it through the glass.

Nothing. She might as well have been shining the torch into a bottomless pit for all the good it did. Rather than dwell on the thought she turned her attention to the corridor ahead of her.

And almost screamed when she saw what was written on the wall.

It couldn't be blood, she kept telling herself, as her torch traced the smeary red letters. And most of all it couldn't be Morrie's blood.

AT MIDNIGHT I WILL STEAL YOUR SOUL

She shuddered. He *must* have heard that doctor say it. That could be the only explanation. She did her best to shut out the part of her brain that kept insisting

Morrie couldn't possibly have written those words, partly because they were too high, but mainly because it looked as if someone had used a paintbrush rather than a grimy finger.

There was a noise behind her, from far down the corridor. A kind of scratching, croaking sound that she didn't like at all. Holding the pen torch before her, its narrow beam thankfully not broad enough to remind her of what was on the wall to her left, Lynda began to retrace her steps as swiftly as she could.

It wasn't long before she reached a right turn, which was odd as she distinctly remembered coming down a short flight of steps just before she had arrived at the room. She must have been mistaken, she thought, but she hadn't gone much further before she became convinced there was something wrong. She certainly hadn't come through a hospital ward on the way here. A ward with peeling yellow paint on its cracked walls, its floor strewn with chunks of plaster and other detritus.

There were noises either side of her. Rustlings, as if blankets were being moved and sheets being rumpled. She held the torch as high as she could and looked around.

There were ten cots, lined up against either side of the ward, and it was only when she took a step forward that she realised that was where the noises were coming from. Beneath the stained, tattered tartan blanket of each cot lay a shape, a shape that clawed at its coverings, gurgling in a way that no normal child was ever meant to.

Lynda took a deep breath and walked as quickly as she could to the ward's far end, chancing, as she passed the final cot on the left, to see a mottled fleshy protuberance emerge from beneath the sheet, the hideous squawk that accompanied it making her move all the faster.

Her heart was hammering again and she forced herself to take deep breaths to try and calm herself, to not think about the ghosts of the things she had just left behind, what Dr Wellington had referred to as the 'deformed and the destitute'. The air that filled her lungs and nostrils was musty and dust-filled, and there was something else as well. A reek of infirmity and decay. She had only ever smelt something like it once before, when as a little girl she had been taken to visit her grandmother in a care home shortly before the old woman had died of the cancer that had been eating away at her insides.

It was the odour of the nearly dead.

She shone the torch ahead of her, preferring to face whatever was in this new room than be left guessing at what the darkness might be hiding.

At first she thought she was in amongst more children – older ones this time. But then she realised the hunched forms in the beds grasped their sheets with twisted arthritic fingers, what little hair they had on their scabrous scalps a dirty grey colour in the dim light.

She was three steps closer to the way out when one of them spoke to her.

"Are you my mummy?" the ancient crone whispered, the child-like quality of her voice causing Lynda to stop. Next to the woman's bed, taped to the scratched pine box that passed for a bedside table, was a photograph of an attractive woman in her early thirties. As Lynda looked about her she realised all the patients had them. Each of these demented, dying old women had been provided with a picture of how they must have looked in their youth.

"Are you my mummy?" the old lady croaked again. "I think I'm late for school."

Lynda bit her lip.

62

"There's no school today," she eventually managed to say.

"Really?"

"No. Now go back to sleep."

By now her face was streaked with tears, her insides were churning and her heart was thumping so hard her ribs ached.

How many times since she had been made to visit her grandmother in that awful place had she worried she might end up like one of the women she was now looking at? A gibbering demented wreck with no control over her movements and no memory of those who should have been familiar to her, treating them with confusion and then aggression as she soiled herself once more and had to be wheeled away by a care assistant whose only response was 'She does that a lot. It's not your fault.' And now here she was, confronting yet another nightmare.

She paused, suddenly realising something. These *were* her nightmares.

Being imprisoned in a lunatic asylum, having nothing better to do with the rest of her life than waiting to die, perhaps killing herself by slashing her throat rather than marry that imbecile Pete and having a child even more retarded than he was. Or ending up on her own, old, demented and afraid, wishing that any random visitor to the long-stay ward on which she was to remain forever was her mother rather than the ineffectual harridan who had scared her so much, even if it was unwittingly, when she was a child.

All the things she had seen. They were all her nightmares.

As if everything from the moment she had seen that twisted dwarf thing had been staged especially for her.

By whatever it was that was haunting this dreadful place.

The thing that was taking an awful lot of time and trouble to make a good job of scaring her to death.

"I wonder what you are," she said aloud, the sound of her voice giving her confidence. "Are you like I was – a child who just never got hugged enough? Or are you old? So old and so weary of what the world did to you that you want to revisit some of your pain back on me? Or are you something else entirely? Something weird and wrong? Something I won't ever be able to reason with?" And then, remembering what her father had once said, "Or are you just smoke and mirrors?"

As she talked, she sensed a dark shape beginning to take form behind her. Initially small and dwarf-like, it gradually swelled to become a cloak of blackness that towered over her. A scythe-shaped blade of darkness emerged from its left side and prepared to hook itself around her throat.

"I know you're behind me," she said.

The shape hesitated, the single razor-sharp black talon held in mid-air as she turned to face whatever it was.

"So you've decided to show yourself to me, even though you're actually still hiding, aren't you?" she said.

The shape did nothing.

"You see I know a lot about hiding," she said. "Because I've been doing it all of my life. In fact you could say I'm a bit of an expert. Hiding my feelings, hiding my ambitions, hiding my potential, all because I've been so shit scared of everything I haven't dared imagine that if I face up to what terrifies me there's just the chance that I might not come off worst. Or rather worse, there being only two of us and worse being the right word to use. And Mrs McMasters said I never learned anything in her English class. Maybe she wasn't such a shit teacher after all."

The shape remained silent. Maybe it couldn't talk. Well now she was on a roll she wasn't going to stop.

"Do you know, I even drove the wrong way to get to this bloody place? And when I think about it, I mean *really* think, it feels as if I've been going the wrong way for a lot of my life, too. Trying to make other people happy when I should have been thinking about myself for a change. And it's never occurred to me to try and turn round. Until now. The real pain in the arse is that I've only just realised it, and it's far too late because whoever or whatever you are, you're going to kill me."

"It does not matter what I am or who I was."

The thing's voice was ethereal – both deliciously comforting and maliciously untrustworthy at the same time. The kind of voice you could let lull you to sleep as its owner prepared to twist a knife between the bones of your spine. "What matters is what I can do for you. In return, of course, for what you can do for me."

"And what is that?" said Lynda, standing her ground. If she was going to die anyway she was damned if it was going to be reduced to the kind of blubbering mess she sometimes used to end up in at school.

Now the shape raised both its 'arms' wide as if to embrace her in its cloak of nothingness.

"Those whom you have left behind are still imprisoned," it said.

Lynda peered at what passed for the figure's torso, and at the image forming upon it. An image of those still trapped in the rehearsal room, appearing to have given up all hope as the air began to run out in the sealed chamber.

"You can give it back to them," said the voice. "You can give them hope and set them free."

"How?"

Lynda had a horrible feeling she knew but she had to ask anyway. The answer wasn't long in coming. Two words that turned her insides into a crawling mass of dread.

"Be mine."

She looked again at the prisoners in the room, then at her surroundings. Her rotting, crumbling surroundings. Nameless terrors waited for her in every nook and cranny, behind every door and window.

In every second between every breath she took.

"Why?" she breathed.

"Fear nourishes me, loathing feeds me, horror sustains me such that when I am replete it fills me with sensations more overpoweringly delicious than anything you can possibly imagine experiencing with that body of yours. Anything. And you have so much horror within you, and are capable of so much more. Stay here, with me. Be my sustenance. You are so much better suited to it than the pathetic examples who have been locked up in this miserable place, the ones I came here to seek out and whom I hoped I might fill myself to the brim with from their fears until I was overflowing. But their petty neuroses and witless phobias are but scraps compared to you – someone who has lived with fear all her life, someone who can find terror in the slightest breath of wind, misinterpret a single word to assume the person who has spoken it means you harm, make every action you take something you feel you should be blamed for. Be mine. You will suffer endlessly, but the freedom of those whom I now have trapped will provide you with some comfort that perhaps for once in your miserable life you have done something that is actually worthwhile."

Lynda closed her eyes but she could still see the shape, and the room, and the people in it. What should she do? Let them all die? Or give herself up to this thing? She who *had* never done anything worthwhile in her life, who *had* always been afraid, who *had* always been unable to look on the bright side, to make the most of the occasional opportunities that had come her way. She who *had* never been truly happy, had never been truly ecstatic.

Had never even been in love.

She took a deep breath, clenched her fists, and looked up at the creature as it continued to tower over her. It took all her courage, all her stamina to say the words, and they almost came out as a stammer. But they didn't, and that just gave her all the more strength.

"Fuck. Off."

The creature let out a booming laugh, in a voice completely unlike the calming, seductive one of moments ago. This one was distinctly unpleasant, self-confident, forceful. The kind someone well-versed in physical abuse might use, Lynda thought.

"Do you really think you have a choice?" the thing roared.

Yes, she thought. I must do, or you wouldn't be pissing about here playing silly buggers. You'd have raped my heart and stolen my soul the minute I entered this place. Before I even had a chance to know you were here you'd have turned me into your willing terror slave, and you haven't.

Which means you can't.

Which means you can fuck off.

"I think I've had enough of this now," she said. "In fact I think it's time for me to leave."

She made to walk past the shadow. It blocked her way.

"They will die." It hissed at her.

"So what if they do?" she said. "Why should I care? Apart from one, I hadn't met any of them until this evening. And you already know I was far too scared to actually talk to any of them. They talked to me, or rather at me, because that's all anyone ever does. Now get out of my way. I'm bored with you, and with all of this, and as a matter of fact I am bored to death with my life, but if I am going to die here and if I am going to die now you can fuck off if you think I'm going to let it do you any good in the process."

She walked straight forward into concentrated evil, into the absolute blackness that had been pursuing her in this hospital because she had lived the kind of life that had made it possible for this thing to desire her, to stalk her, to wish to possess her.

There was a brief moment of darkness, a brief sensation of chill, a brief taste of something sickly sweet, tempting and yet oozing with insidious corruption, and then she was on the other side of it. Beyond it. She freed her hair from the constricting band that had been holding it in place and ran her fingers through tresses damp with sweat. And as she did so she realised that she felt different.

No, not different exactly.

Herself.

More herself than she had ever felt
before. More in touch with herself, more
in touch with her desires, more in touch
with the sort of person she wanted to be.
Walking through that thing of shadow had
caused her to lose something, certainly.
But it had been her anxieties, her
inhibitions, other things that her new self
felt she was probably better off without
anyway.

And she had gained so much more.

She turned round to see what was left
of the thing that had so terrified her, but
it had gone. Perhaps she had killed it,
perhaps it had moved onto pastures new.

Perhaps it had never really been there in the first place.

But she was there, feeling vibrant and bloody and new.

Bloody?

She hadn't noticed it before but the front of her blouse was stained with the stuff. She checked her arms, and her throat. Nothing. Someone else's then. Perhaps even the creature's. She pulled the sticky material away from her skin, running reddened fingers across herself to push the bloodstained material away from her, and began to walk back the way she had come. A different person and yet somehow the same. A better person? For herself, certainly, but not necessarily for anyone else.

Oh no.

It was time for her to start getting what she wanted out of life, and at that moment all the fear, all the anxiety, all the panic she had ever felt had been converted into an almost uncontainable rage against the stultifying normality of those whose lives had made her own seem so inadequate.

She was almost ready to start her new life, but first she needed to get rid of all those negative emotions. All that hate, all that anger, all that suppressed violence.

She found she was holding the key to the rehearsal room in one hand, and the kind of knife that could be used to skin a cow in the other. She gripped both with a sense of delicious anticipation she had never before experienced, and which she felt, if she was not careful, could become addictive.

People like unhappy endings, Dr Wellington had said.

She set off to give them exactly what they wanted.

About the Author

John Llewellyn Probert was the winner of the 2013 British Fantasy Award for best novella with *The Nine Deaths of Dr Valentine*. He won the Dracula Society's Children of the Night Award for his first book, *The Faculty of Terror*, in 2006. Since then he has published fifteen volumes of horror fiction, including six short story collections.

His non-fiction publications include a book on his favourite film, *Theatre of Blood* (Electric Dreamhouse) and he regularly writes about new movie releases at his online review site, *House of Mortal Cinema*.

He lives in a gothic mansion in deepest Somerset with his wife, the author Thana Niveau. He doesn't sleep much because there's just too much scary fun to be had.

Also by
John Llewellyn Probert

Nine Deaths of Dr Valentine

The Lovecraft Squad

The Last Temptations of Dr Valentine

The Complete Valentine

Theatre of Blood

... and more.

We would like to thank everyone who
made this project possible,
via the Kickstarter and outside of it.

Specific thanks goes to:

Aaron Armitage

David Parker

Ross Warren

More dyslexic friendly

titles coming soon...

BOTH
PUBLISHING